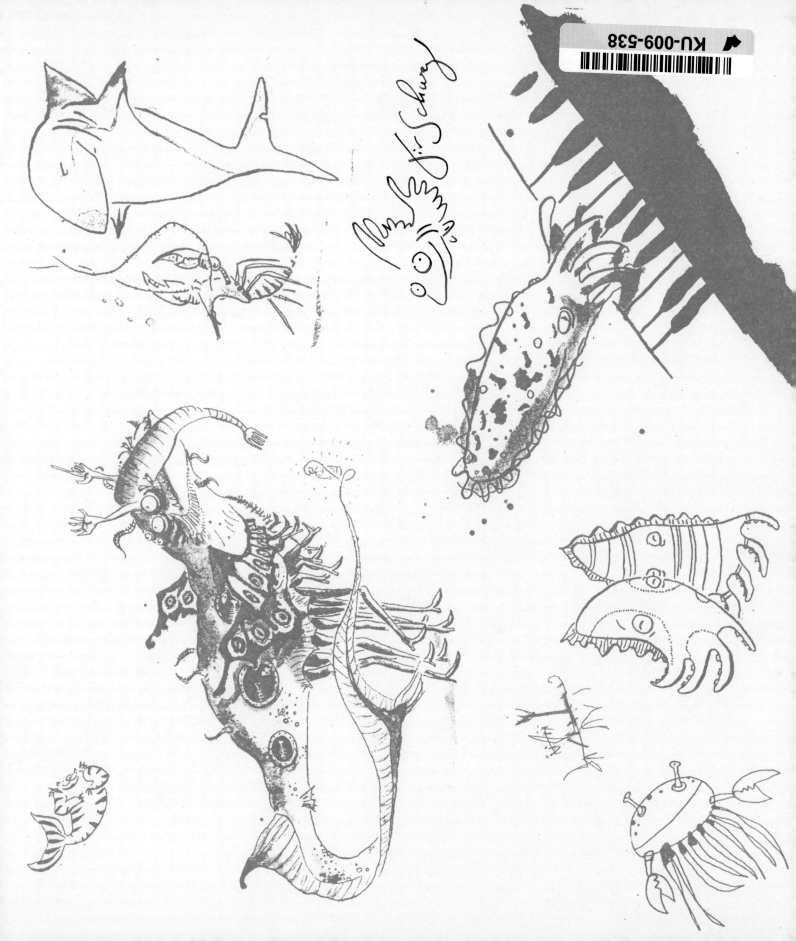

SHARK AND LOBSTER'S

Amazing Undersea Adventure

Written and drawn by
Viviane Schwarz

coloured by
Joel Stewart

First published 2006 by Walker Books Ltd
87 Vauxhall Walk, London SE11 5HJ

10 9 8 7 6 5 4 3 2 1

British Library Cataloguing in
Publication Data: a catalogue
record for this book is available
from the British Library

ISBN-13: 978-0-7445-8899-6
ISBN-10: 0-7445-8899-5

www.walkerbooks.co.uk

for Mel
V. S.

WALKER BOOKS

AND SUBSIDIARIES

LONDON • BOSTON • SYDNEY • AUCKLAND

TIGERS!

A very small cuttlefish had been watching...

Five minutes later,
the small cuttlefish
had fetched her family
and friends,
and her friends' families,
and some very spiky crabs.

They brought seven hundred
rocks and a piano.
Now they had walls.
The cuttlefish played the
piano and Lobster danced
with the crabs.

Shark pulled a face
and coughed.
Then he sang:

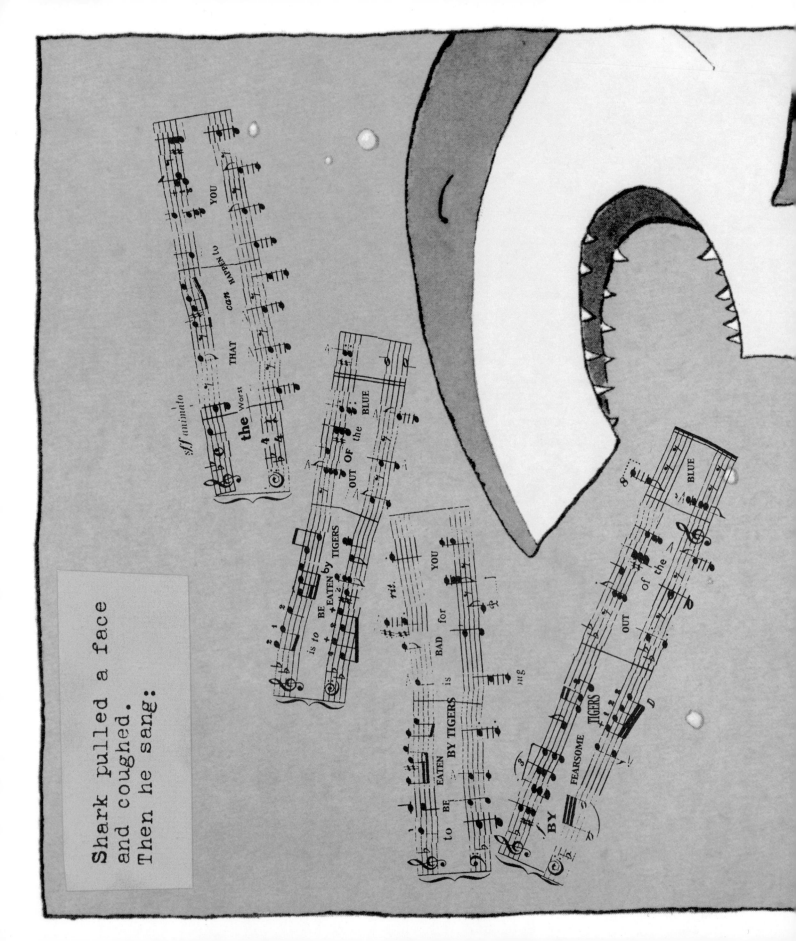

Everyone fell silent and looked around.
There was blue everywhere.

Maybe our fortress isn't big enough.

There was a great clattering as the spiky crabs shivered with fright.

So they all went
down into the
deep sea,
and diving
tumbling
and sinking.

They didn't have to look for long.
There was a huge big monster,
stretched out as far as they could see.
Its mouth was wide enough to eat
a whale sideways.

Where's the END of it?

THE SMALLEST DOT OF LIGHT OUT IN THE DARK, THAT'S THE LANTERN ON THE END OF MY TAIL...

And look at all the EYES!

I'VE GOT SEVEN AND A FEW...

Look at all the LEGS!

I'VE GOT EIGHT THOUSAND AND TWO...

Together
they carried
the sleeping
monster
up from
the deep
sea...

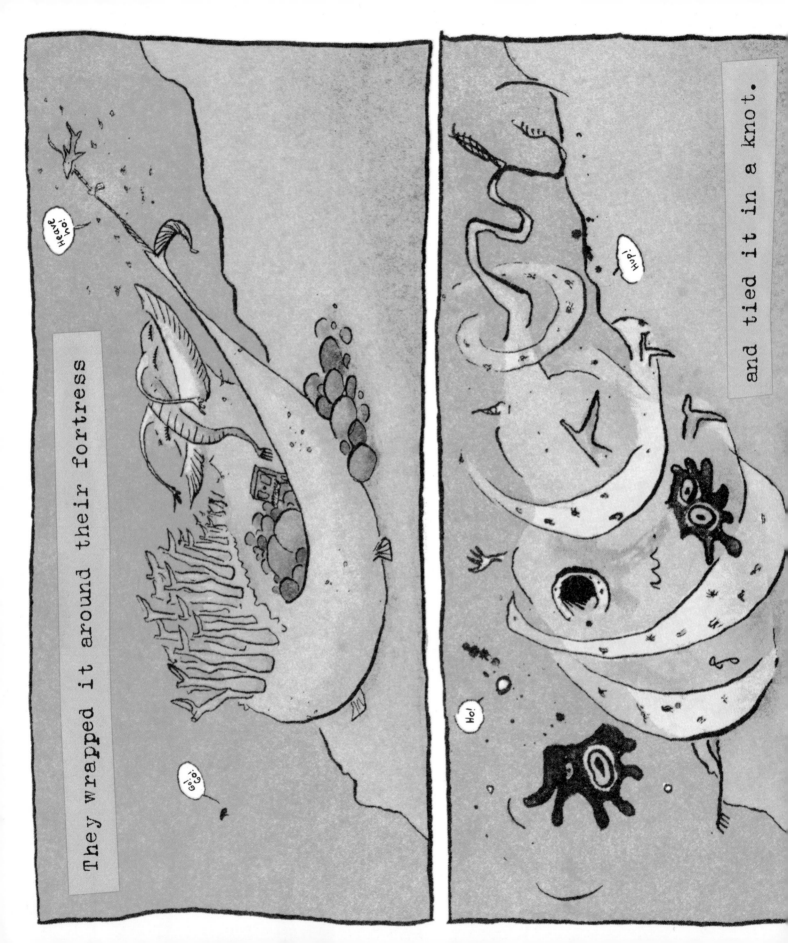

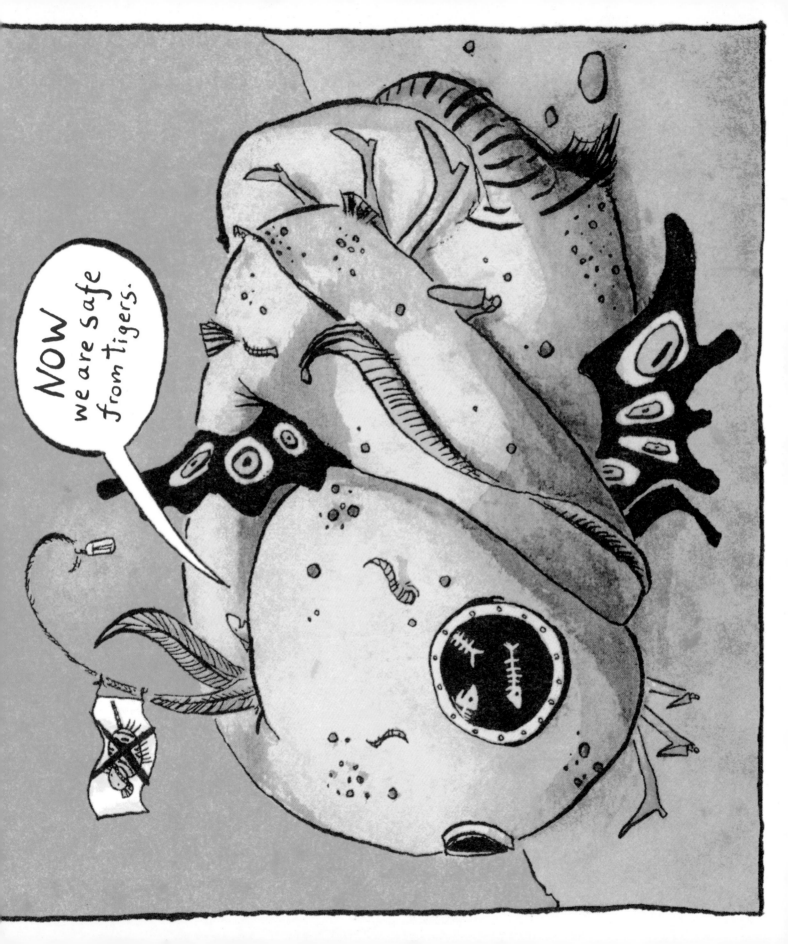

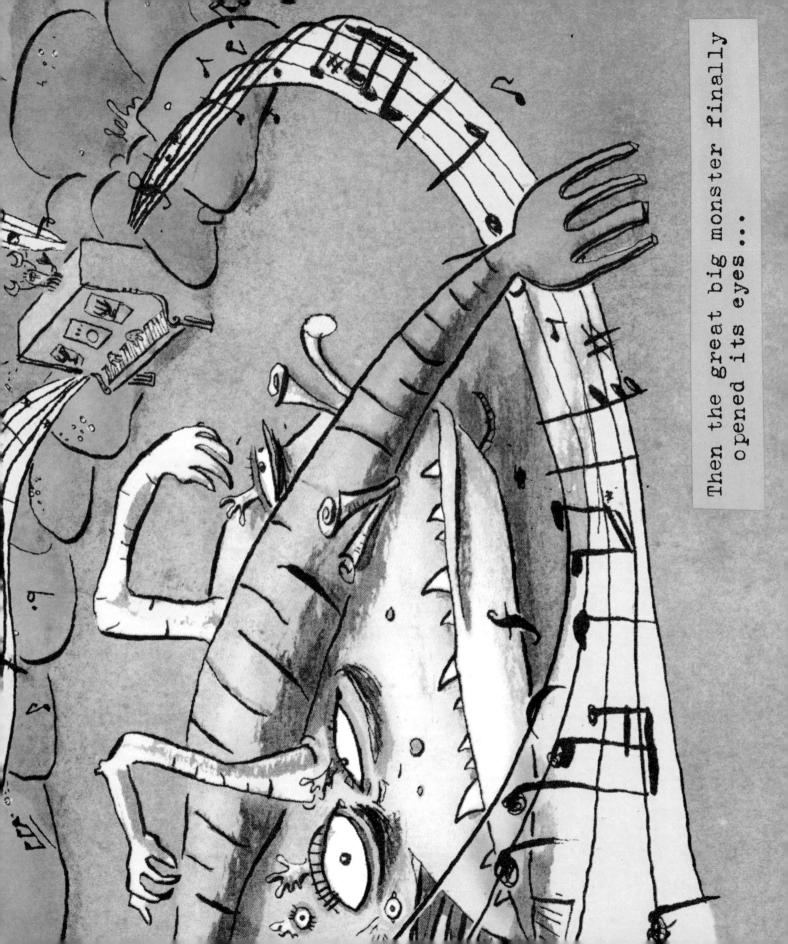

Then the great big monster finally opened its eyes ...

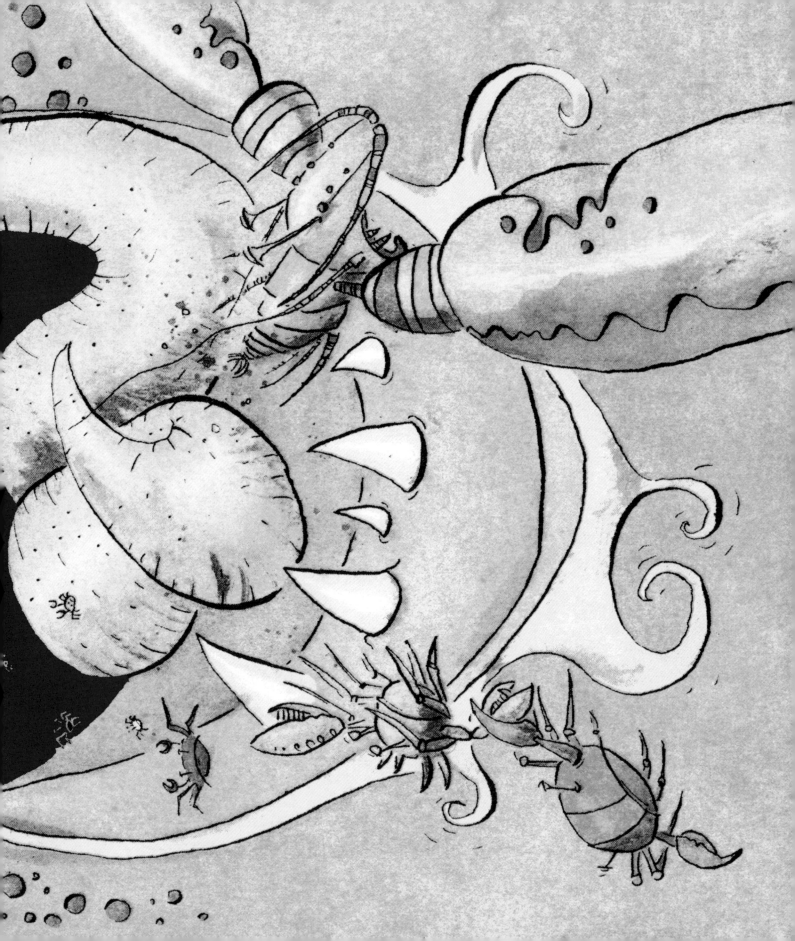

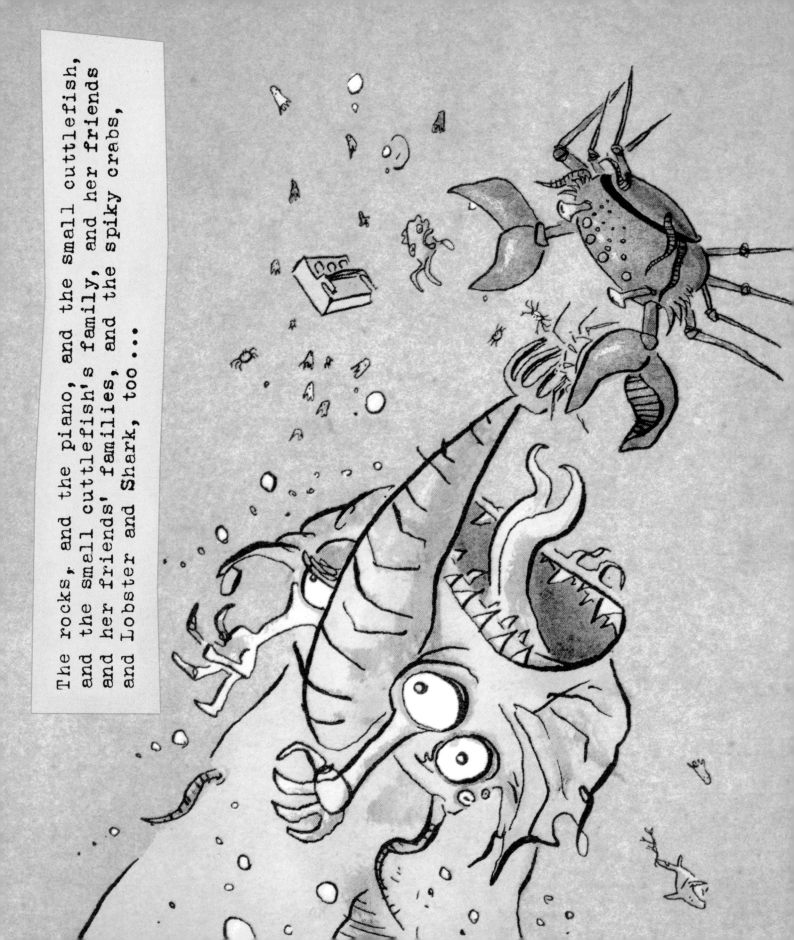

The rocks, and the piano, and the small cuttlefish, and the small cuttlefish's family, and her friends and her friends' families, and the spiky crabs, and Lobster and Shark, too ....

and around
and around . . . .

and
down . . . .

and up . . . .

were chased
left and
right . . . .

until they were scattered all over the ocean . . . .

and the monster was tired and
went back to the deep sea.

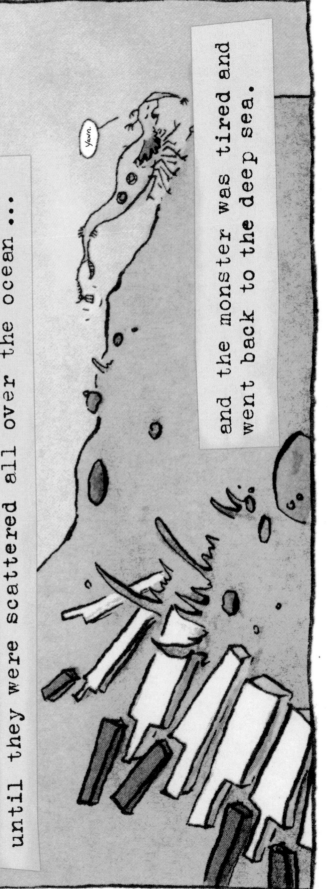

They
were safe
at last.

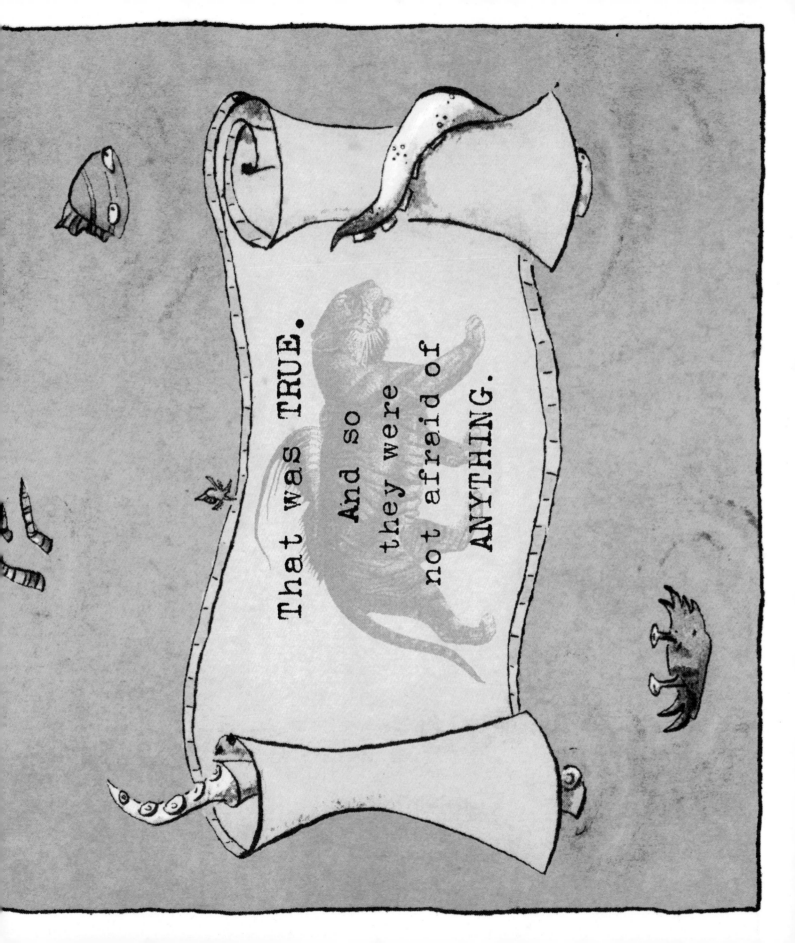